**Do these a** **your child**

MW00812284

See It, Say It

Ask your child to color the star beside the word when he or she finds it in the book.

Make sure your child understands what each word means.

☆ inventor ☆ explorer

☆ onions ☆ volcanoes

Does It Fit?

Help your child read these words out loud.

Then say, *Some of these words have the same sound at the beginning. Cross out three words that have a different beginning sound.*

trees   caves   jungles
camels   doctor   hippos

To, With, and By

To	Read four pages out loud *to* your child. Run your finger under the words as you say them at a normal speed. Make sure your child is looking at the words.
With	Read the same four pages out loud *with* your child. Run your finger under the words as you say them at a normal speed. Your child will probably say every other word correctly.
By	Run your finger under the words as your child says them *by* himself or herself. Help your child fix any mistakes.

Continue doing *To, With, and By* a few pages at a time for the rest of this book. Have your child reread this story for the next several days until it sounds great and is practically memorized.

 Go to www.RocketReaders.com for more reading tips.

Faith Kidz® is an imprint of Cook Communications Ministries
Colorado Springs, Colorado 80918
Cook Communications, Paris, Ontario
Kingsway Communications,
Eastbourne, England

WHAT WILL YOU BE?
©2003 by Cook Communications

First printing, 2003
Printed in Korea
1 2 3 4 5 6 7 Printing/Year 07 06 05 04 03

Senior Editor: Heather Gemmen
Design Manager: Jeffrey P. Barnes
Designer: Nancy L. Haskins

What Will You Be?

Rocket Readers Level 4

Written by

Heather Gemmen

and

Mary McNeil

Illustrated by

Isidre Mones

Chapter 1

Genesis 45

Joseph
(Jo-sef)

Joseph, what do you want to be when you grow up?

Do you want to be a great explorer?
Will you climb mountains?
Will you find volcanoes?
Will you hike deserts?

Will you climb trees?
Will you find caves?
Will you hike jungles?

Do you want to be an inventor?

Will you make a way to fly in the sky?
Will you make a way to land on the moon?
Will you make a way to dive to the bottom?

Joseph, you grew up.

I grew up to be a boss.
God used me to feed his people.
God used me to lead his people.
God used me to save his people.

Chapter 2

Exodus 15:20

Miriam
(Meer-ee-um)

Miriam, what do you want to be when you grow up?

Do you want to be a zookeeper?
Will you feed the zebras?
Will you ride the camels?
Will you water the giraffes?

Will you feed the peacocks?
Will you ride the elephants?
Will you water the hippos?

Miriam, you grew up.

I grew up to be a prophet.
God used me to sing his praises.
God used me to lead his people.
God used me to speak his words.

Chapter 3

Judges 4

Deborah
(Deb-ruh)

Deborah, what do you want to be when you grow up?

Do you want to be an artist?
Will you make a bowl?
Will you paint a picture?
Will you write a poem?

Will you make a rug?
Will you paint a pot?
Will you write a song?

Do you want to be a doctor?

Will you help sick people get well?
Will you help hurt people get strong?
Will you help sad people get happy?

Deborah, you grew up.

I grew up to be a judge.
God used me to speak his words.
God used me to lead his people.
God used me to save his people.

Chapter 4

2 Samuel 2:4

David
(Day-vid)

David, what do you want to be when you grow up?

Do you want to be a cook?
Will you boil eggs?
Will you grill onions?
Will you bake muffins?

Will you boil spaghetti?
Will you grill lamb chops?
Will you bake cakes?

David, you grew up.

I grew up to be a king.
God used me to sing his praises.
God used me to lead his people.
God used me to save his people.

What Will You Be?

Life Issue: I want my child to learn God has a purpose for him or her.

Spiritual Building Block: Purpose

Do the following activities to help your child know God has a purpose:

Sight: Get out a family photo album. Show your child pictures of you as a child. Talk about the things you dreamed of as a child. Tell your child how God showed you his plan at an important time in your life.

Sound: Ask your child to give endings to these sentences:

When David grew up, God helped him become a _____.

If I were a doctor, God would help me do things like _____.

When I grow up, I want to be a _____.

Touch: Have your child write these words from Jeremiah 29:11 in the lines below:

"I know the plans I have for you," declares the Lord.